The Bathing Huts

The Bathing Huts

Monique Lange

translated by
Barbara Beaumont

MARION BOYARS . LONDON . NEW YORK

Published in Great Britain and the United States in 1986
by Marion Boyars Publishers Ltd.
24 Lacy Road, London SW15 1NL and
262 West 22nd Street, New York, NY 10011.

Distributed in the United States by
The Scribner Book Companies Inc.

Distributed in Canada by
Collier Macmillan Canada Inc.

Distributed in Australia by
Wild & Woolley Pty Ltd.

Distributed in New Zealand by
Benton Ross

Published originally under the title *Les Cabines de Bain*
by Editions Gallimard, Paris, in 1982

© Editions Gallimard, 1982

© This translation Marion Boyars Publishers, 1986

British Library Cataloguing in Publication Data

Lange, Monique
   The bathing huts.
   I. Title   II. Les Cabines de bain. *English*
   843'.914 [F]   PQ2672.A52

Library of Congress Cataloging in Publication Data

Lange, Monique.
   The bathing huts.

   Translation of: Les cabines de bain.
   I. Title.
PQ2672.A52C2513 1985   843'.914   84-29287

ISBN 0-7145-2821-8   cloth

Typeset in 12/14 point Baskerville by Essex Photo Set, Rayleigh
Printed and bound in Great Britain
at The Camelot Press plc, Southampton

For Joe

For Odette

About the book

Sent by her doctor to recuperate from an illness in Roscoff, Brittany, the 'young woman', reflects on the failed relationships and wasted potentialities that have left her stranded and alone. She is writing a diary that will return the past to her intact, but Roscoff is full of old people, the tide is perpetually out and conference delegates wander aimlessly along the grey sand. Painful memories rob her of sleep. She is haunted by friends who have died, by her husband's homosexual lovers and 'Mitterand being shifty on television'.

Overwhelmed by loss and despair, her sense of humour and human possibility is rekindled by an odd, sensual relationship with a seventy year old man whom she meets by chance. *The Bathing Huts* combines the moments of self-discovery of an intimate journal and the craft of a finely wrought work of fiction. It speaks with a voice all its own, in a language that is both colloquial and highly charged. This fascinating short novel will resonate in the mind of every woman who has grown older without realizing it.

About the author

Monique Lange was born in Paris and spent her childhood in Indo-China. Her work has evoked comparison with the best of Simone de Beauvoir and Françoise Sagan. She lives in Paris and works as a scriptwriter. *The Bathing Huts* is her seventh novel and the third to be translated into English.

I

The doctor told her: 'I see Brittany as the only solution for you. I think Roscoff will do you a lot of good'.

This doctor, whom she didn't know – her own doctor was dead, his successor also – seems rather bored, at most a little worried, as he looks at her.

He is sitting opposite her. She would like to like him. But she can't. She looks at his desk. It is Empire style. At least she thinks so, she is no longer sure of anything. It would be a style she hates. She wonders if he writes anything else besides prescriptions on it.

Now he says: 'You can get dressed again.'

The young woman has never been to Brittany and this doctor whom she doesn't know decides to exile her to Roscoff.

She recalls all the sunny places she has been to. With him. With them. She has always loved the sun. She has never suffered from the heat. She has never suffered from the cold either. Her relationship with nature is a good one – good until today, when this stranger whom she dislikes intensely chose Brittany for her.

She sees again the sun and the south that she has loved so

11

much. She has been there with the father of her daughter and later with her husband.

She remembers their happiness at Capri. Her daughter is still very young, indescribably delightful. The island seems to be made for her. They go off in a rowing boat to fish for sea-urchins and to drink vin rosé. The fisherman says that the rounder sea-urchins are the females. They can be recognized by a tiny shred of sea-weed that they cling on to as if it were a mink stole. The fisherman would exclaim: 'Oh! the vain things' or 'Oh! the little hussies'.

And then she pictures them on another island, Hvar in Yugoslavia. Her daughter is still very young. She helps the secretary to type the hotel menus on an old typewriter. There is teleci at every meal. Teleci is veal.

And she remembers Venice, still with them. There is a summer storm. She runs with her daughter beneath the beating rain. He is furious. She remembers the striptease in the vast corridors of the Hotel Excelsior – before reaching their rooms – as if to get their own back on wasted time.

She sees the sun of Spain, inseparable from the crimson of the Civil War, the crimson of ecclesiastical vestments, the crimson of the bullfight.

Then that pink village where all is exposed to public gaze and yet so full of surprises in winter. They lived there for two years after the death of her mother. She remembers her powerful feelings, the same each time that they caught their first glimpse of the village, still there in all its pinkness, as they rounded the bend a few kilometres past Saint-Maxime. It was so beautiful that it seemed a miracle, a mirage.

Almost in spite of herself, this village inspired in her a kind thought for someone she really despised, but who had said that whenever he reached this bend in the road, he would stop his car, get out and kiss the ground and set off again. That man had fallen passionately in love with the pink village at about the same time as herself and he had left it too.

And this unknown doctor was sending her to Brittany, to Roscoff, to the end of the world.

II

Roscoff, the only thing she likes about it is its Russian sounding name. She also feels the need to travel.

He has set off for Carboneras, Murcia, Almeria. He is on the road to Marrakesh or Damascus, Tiznit, Istanbul, Palmyra, to Zagora, to Oujda, in the desert of El-Golea. From her daughter she has received letters posted in London, Rome, Pondicherry, New Delhi, Goa, New York, Los Angeles, Lima, Mexico.

And she remembers two addresses with a French ring to them: Richelieu Towers in Montreal and the rue Molière in Tangier.

Both of them write in telegraphic style: 'Been raining since yesterday, am reading Diderot from morning till night.' 'Returned exhausted from my trip to the Sahara.' Seen some lamps and plates that will buy for you when back in Istanbul.' 'The real thing for me is New York and getting ready to go to California.' 'The monsoon has started, not too troublesome.' 'Great innovation, had my hair cut in Los Angeles.'

But her first husband, the father of her daughter, used to write in a hermetic style. 'Knowing where we are going

14

matters little, whether our boat be a gondola or not, you are dearer to me than any creature on earth.'

Her travels had begun with him.

She remembers their first trip to the south. Before they had always gone to his parents in Alsace. That summer, they had left their three month old daughter with them.

She remembers especially her extraordinary joy when he had told her, as they were driving through Avignon or Orange (the motorway was not yet built at that time): 'I've given the keys of our flat to J. Do you know who's making love in our daughter's bedroom?' No. And he had said the name of a woman they both liked a lot and she had been wanton enough to conceal an affair in her dear rue Poissonnière (her house) – which, like so many other houses, would see couples come together and drift apart.

Her first trip to Spain had been with the father of her daughter. A portent of the whole of her life, of what she might call her fate, on condition she did not complain about it. She remembered having breakfast at Villajoyosa with former 'heroes' of the Civil War, her childish admiration for the Spanish people and their boundless generosity, hospitality and cruelty. Then they (like them) had carried on as far as Morocco. They had ferried their second-hand Simca Five across the Mediterranean; at the time that car seemed like an outrageous symbol of wealth. They (like them) had landed at Tangier.

This was the time when she was attracted to Spain (and Spaniards) after reading Hemingway's *Death in the Afternoon*.

She had inflicted pangs of jealousy on her first husband by throwing a gold plated necklace to a torero in Bayonne one Sunday afternoon. A year later, he was to leave her for

15

another woman, but for a long time she would cling to clichés, wrong notions, from which she would only gradually free herself, and that only through a form of suffering.

But the traces do vanish. Already twenty years have passed. Perhaps more. They have all gone. Gone for one reason or another. Gone to one place or another. That's what life must be about: getting used to people leaving you.

Later the young woman will know the sweetness when people return, that those who leave do sometimes come back. It is, above all, everyday life that seems ill-suited to living.

III

When the young woman arrives at Roscoff, she feels completely disorientated. She has been looking at fields of artichokes since Morlaix. She sees them as clenched fists threatening her.

At the station are more round shapes, pink and blue hydrangeas. These blooms are also like thrusting fists, and the young woman has no strength to fight back.

Roscoff is a small grey village. It will take some getting used to for someone who likes only white. For the first time in her life (should she be sad?) her luggage is light. A taxi drops her in front of the Hotel des Arcades. In the lobby she hears something that should reassure her. One old lady says to another: 'I've been staying at the Arcades for twelve years now. If I weren't satisfied, I wouldn't stay here.' In the state that she is in, the young woman clutches at straws.

She sees a lot of old people. A sea of little old people. It seems strange to her, she who has so much wanted to die, or rather not to live any longer. Will she become a part of this group of little old ladies whose voices she can hear already?

– If you get as far as seventy, you're all right after that.

– My shoulder's not bad, but I've lost all feeling in my neck.

17

– All those things up in space, they can't be doing us any good, you know.

If she is to be a little old lady, she would like not to be a burden to anyone. To be a light and indispensable little old lady.

In fact, that's more or less what she is already.

– But you're not old. You're going through a difficult patch. You'll see, people always come through it.

She hears a man who seems to be still young – judging by these new criteria – saying to a friend.

– My mother has been worrying me this last year, she has gone down hill a lot.

– How old is she? asks the friend, visibly thinking only of his own sufferings.

– She'll be a hundred on 14 July.

An angel flies over Roscoff. The young woman, in the depths of her despair, cannot hold back a smile.

IV

When the young woman opens the shutters of her room, she sees the sea. Or rather a soggy desert. The tide is a long way out. It's strange. She has not seen that before. When she was younger, she had the sea at her feet.

She sees men dressed in navy blue walking on the sand like penguins. She is to learn from the hotel proprietress that they are conference delegates. There is a conference in Roscoff. Perhaps a conference for learning how to live again.

She can smell sea-weed and iodine. She breathes in the wind. She knows nothing about Roscoff. It's better that way. She must unlearn everything. That's the only way she can pick up her life again.

The young woman has asked for a double room. She doesn't really know why or for whom. She wants to pretend she is not alone.

– I couldn't do it for you in the high season, the lady said.

The young woman reflects sadly on the season for loving.

– Half-board is compulsory.

– Of course, the young woman answers.

She arranges the room as if he were going to come . She tries to control her untidiness that annoys him so much. The father of her daughter, her first husband, also found this lack of order difficult to bear. Even if she makes an omelette, the kitchen is a mess. If she reads a book in bed, she has with her five others that she might just feel like reading. But in this room with its sea-view, though the sea is not there, she is going to try to be tidy. In her life. In her cupboards and in her head.

When she has got her strength back and is able to return to the rue Poissonnière, she will tidy her bookshelves. Here again, it is established order that upsets her. She refuses to classify things alphabetically. She wants to arrange her books with fervour and according to their affinities. But is she sure she is right to put James next to Pavese and Fitzgerald next to Hemingway who didn't like him and was very cruel towards him?

There is delight in being arbitrary. She is mistress of her library. The joy, the pain that certain books have given her. As the world opened up it was nearly always like a wound, or an act of revolt. She hadn't looked for reassurance in books either. She remembers the turning point in her life that reading Genêt had been. It gave her access to a world that would always be closed to her but enabled her to cross a divide. There is a kind of beauty that should bring pain.

The young woman again looks out of the window at the absent sea and its seems as if life also is absent. Yet she loves it too much (life that is). She will find it again; seize hold of it. She doesn't yet know how. But that is why she is there. She is not there to feel sorry for herself. Besides, self-pity is not her style.

V

The young woman walks around Roscoff. She meets little old men all hunched up and red cheeked Breton women (the effect of sea breezes or Calvados)?

There is a stubbornness, a healthiness, something invigorating, not sickly, that ought to reassure her, but she still feels too groggy.

Groggy because they have gone?

No, just groggy.

Groggy also because she can't manage to write.

Not to her friends.

But a book in which she would explain all you have to do in order to be happy and also all that you must not do.

You can read that sort of thing in women's magazines.

You hear it in electoral campaigns and every day on the radio.

'Dear So-and-so, I have this pain. Dear So-and-so, I have that pain.'

There is a ring of truth in all this individual suffering, all this failing, this lack of success.

'I listen to you every night because I haven't been able to sleep for ages.'

She is starting to think that people who sleep well ought to pay a sleep tax. It's too rare, sleep. It's too hard to experience, to hold on to.

Anything at all can deprive her of sleep. Anyone at all.

A vision of him in the desert.

The noise of her daughter slamming a door.

Mitterand being sly on television.

Joe refusing to show emotion.

O's colourless voice.

Not finding the right sentence. Or word.

She is walking through a new world. The lobsters at the fishmonger's look lively. Not like in the south. There they look as if they have already swum a hunded times round Princess Grace's soup tureen. Coats are buttercup yellow or navy blue. They are 'functional'. Made to be comfortable at sea, to protect from the sea.

We no longer dress in such a purposeful way. The shops are all Unisex now.

But she quite likes walking along the street behind an adolescent, wondering whether it's a boy or a girl.

It is a rather pallid June day. She often used to be in a frenzy in June, on the brink of the holidays. The sun opened up the world for her.

The young woman would like to make a list of all the mistakes that have marked the stages of her life. That would take a good day. But as if she were seeking to hide from her own foolishness – she hasn't come here to suffer – she falls back on conventional wisdom and wants to attribute all blame to that.

It blocked her horizon. The notion of happiness, peace, the notion of injustice as well as the notion of wickedness.

The rich, the poor, the haves, the have nots. The pure, the impure. The beautiful, the ugly. And pleasure. Ah yes! Pleasure. The fusion of one into the other. Such great confusion. On that point she thinks people really told her too many lies. She found herself face to face with her first experience imprisoned in a straightjacket of clichés that did not help her to take those first steps.

She wonders why people say first steps.

Today, when she looks at her grand-daughter – a pink and peaceful little girl making her first attempt at smiles at her mother, smiles that still perhaps have their origin in the stomach – she tries to meet her eyes with the same passion, the same eagerness with which she sought men's eyes when she was younger. To lose oneself in an exchange of looks. Even in the Underground. It makes her smile now. But she is frantic for her grand-daughter to recognize her. Doubtless such recognition will suffice for a little while. She doesn't remember seeking to meet her daughter's eyes so avidly. And God knows (God?) she loved her passionately, still loves her passionately. When she kisses the forehead of her grand-daughter, she encounters an emotion lost so long ago. Her daughter has not kissed her for fifteen years. It's a very long time. She has tried to rid herself of that image in vain, she has to admit that it always rushes back. That refusal stabs at her. Yet she has had to get used to not being anyone's gateway to moral and physical reality.

But if one is such a thing, it must be terrible when one ceases to be. The young woman is used to not being that, and yet she feels they do love her.

VI

When she was ill, they had been greatly afraid of losing her. That haemorrhage was providential. A testing of love in the fullest sense. One needs to go from 4,500,000 red corpuscles to 1,500,000 to establish it. It's really worth it, especially if the blood count recovers afterwards.

This illness was the catalyst in something strange. After twenty years of living together, he proposed to her. Neither of them believed in marriage. Her rejection of marriage was perhaps a fear of things deteriorating, but they had deteriorated before that. She was bowled over by the thought that, being totally without resources as they were, he could give her nothing but his name. And the house in Spain that he shared with his brothers. Along what secret paths did he wish the daughter of her daughter – not yet born – to run in this garden, as he had run there with them?

They got married on 17 August. It was a number she liked. A few days earlier, she had been walking in Paris and by chance passed by the hospital where her mother had died and she found herself in tears, murmuring to her aloud, on her own in the street: 'Mummy, I'm getting married; Mummy, I'm getting married.'

24

Perhaps the young woman's sadness today is quite simply linked to her body and, when she has got her strength back, order will be restored.

It is precicely this order that she doesn't like. She is rather a messy person. Even in her affections. There are eternal values and transient things, but she likes to find new things, their spoken and unspoken meanings, their secrets, their mysteries, their lies.

People always make fun of her because of her love of human company. It's true that people interest her more than books, nature and music. She likes everything to be related to human beings. The extraordinary landscape that she can see from her windows in Spain, those pine trees and cork-oaks as far as the eye can see, evoke for her her first emotional reaction in the south, and his childhood, when he was hiding in these mountains with his brothers during the Civil War, and they ate chestnuts and swedes. It was while out getting food in Barcelona that their mother – whose eyes were blue like the sunlit waters of a lake – had been killed in an air raid by Franco's troops. That was the first explanation for something that was going to tear them up for life.

She had already been paying for this wound for twenty five years. Paying for. A nasty expression. To pay with oneself. The young woman – who can't find the words she wants – looks for another that means the same thing. Perhaps she'll find it at Roscoff.

VII

When she gets to the beach, the young woman is quite simply indignant. It's a nasty little cove and the sea is far away.

Everyone is wearing big sweaters over their bathing costumes.

But no, when she looks closer, no one is wearing a bathing costume.

Yet the young woman has absolute faith in the sea – even the Breton sea. That's the only thing that can regenerate her.

As she gets undressed, she sees herself in the south once again, sliding off her green tunic.

– You are immodesty itself.

– I see no harm. My immodesty is my way of overcoming my lack of self-confidence. My immodesty is my link with liberty.

Only other people can give you that confidence. . . But they always take it back again!

The young woman shivers now.

– I see Brittany as the only solution for you.

For the moment she can see nothing.

An emaciated old man comes up to her.

– You can get undressed in my hut if you like. It's in the second row. It's very well sheltered.

The young woman looks at him amazed: she has the impression he is speaking in riddles. She turns round and sees bathing huts all lined up like dolls' houses, white and grey huts looking out to sea.

– Your hut?

– I'm a native of Roscoff. I own a hut. I'd be delighted to lend it to you.

The old man is very thin. He looks like Clemenceau. The same thinness as her husband's father and all the beggars they met at Marrakesh.

His glance is blue. A blue eye. Two blue eyes. Of the blue she likes.

– I'd be very happy to be of service to you. Is it your first visit to Roscoff?

– Yes, the young woman answers, it's even my first visit to Brittany.

– Ah, it takes you by surprise, that's for sure, but you'll see, the air is very bracing.

Can she be braced? She wonders. She feels somewhat mummified like those women all done up in bandages that she saw in the museum in Cairo. She is mummified, bound hand and foot, she aches all over. Perhaps it's because she can't manage to tell of her experiences in Egypt. She has nothing left to give. She is dumb. No words, nor gestures.

– Come, I'll show you my hut.

The old man drags the young woman off to his beach hut. There is a rusty key in the door.

– You can leave your things inside. There are no thieves here.

27

The old man is offering her a world without thieves at Roscoff. Just before leaving Paris she got a letter from her Insurance Company informing her that her 'Householder's Comprehensive' was no longer in force. There are so many petty thieves, so many unemployed, that we cannot insure you any longer. Is not this world, forlorn of hope, another of the reasons for her sadness? One cannot always weep for oneself.

In the old man's bathing hut there is, lying on the ground, an old straw-coloured parasol. Three faded blue deck-chairs lean against the wall. Does one talk about the wall of a bathing hut? Yellowed photos are stuck around the edges. The front page of a newspaper with news of the Liberation, a photo of Clemenceau at an angling competition with a very large fish. A photo of a ship: a transatlantic liner. A young woman with pale eyes and a sunshade. A family photo. An old rusty nail with keys hanging on it. Three hooks for clothes. A pile of yellowed old magazines. A photograph of a magnificent negress. Pictures from the colonies. A diploma in sailing. A photo of Danielle Darrieux. A speckled mirror that makes you look like a leopard.

The old man's past is written up on the walls of his hut. She won't ask him any questions. It's her own self that she must be concerned with at the moment. She has no diplomas to show him. She can't even understand how she came to have 'writer' entered on her passport. One should not be prevented from exercising one's profession, especially when it's the only thing one knows how to do.

She wanted to write a story set in Egypt, on the boat that goes up the Nile. She had such clear memories of that journey. So much beauty. A kind of miracle. But she can't get them on to this boat.

She wanted to put on to this boat all the characters she would like to have in a book. And then all the people she loved were to be on it too.

She wanted her daughter to be on it: she loved her with a kind of madness. She was beautiful. She had been a real handful and the young woman had not been prepared for all the anxiety, all the suffering she had gone through on her account. She had sworn never to speak of her until she was out of danger. What did it mean, to be out of danger? It meant: to be wild no more. Her daughter had frightened her with her outrageous appetite for living, her apparent hardness. The young woman used to tell herself that it was *her* fault: she had been too weak, she had been too feeble. She had given the nauseating impression of loving to excess, weeping to excess, being tender to excess.

She wanted him to be on it too, on that boat. She wanted to have him on it because there was something about him that was difficult to hold on to and, once she'd got him on the deck of that boat, he would not shift. And then she had made that journey with him. He used to read *Don Quixote* on deck. It was a very fine journey.

She also wanted her mother and a few other dead people on it, in order to restore them somewhat to life, and then she wanted to put on it all sorts of imaginary characters, but who would resemble people she knew and whom she wanted to talk about.

The June sun is shy. The old man seems shy as well. The young woman is really disorientated.

– I'll wait for you, says the old gentleman.

VIII

The young woman walks towards the sea in her old turquoise bikini. This turquoise was meant for countries with strong colours. It is all worn out. She sometimes even loses the bottom half of it in the sea. . . but she likes it. It has been around too, almost as much as her husband and her daughter. It has been to Capri, Malaga, Saint-Tropez, Corfu, Arenys de Mar. It is familiar with her friend's swimming pool at Carrière-sur-Seine. It has been to Taormina. It has been to Venice. Her little turquoise bikini is well travelled. She'll never throw it away. The turquoise is less bright. It's faded like her.

It's a long way to the sea.

She says to her swimsuit:

– Let me introduce you to Brittany.

The water is cold but it's like a baptism.

I must get used to Brittany, the young woman thinks. I must discover new things. I used to wallow in sun and hot sand. I used to wallow in the light and in received ideas. I used to wallow without knowing it, in my youthfulness, in my vigour. It's not such a bad thing that they have beheaded me.

The young woman starts to swim. It's extraordinary. It's only in the sea that she forgets everything, that she sees everything afresh. This sea that today stings her like a thousand sea-urchins that wish her no harm. She collides with clumps of sea-weed that smell of iodine. She will surely be 'regenerated'. She offers the sea to herself as she did to her child, as she has offered it to other children.

She has retained a love of water from her colonial childhood. It is in the sea that she forgets those things that she doesn't like about herself. The water bears her body. The water conceals her body. The salt baptizes her body. She is going to renovate herself, like her house in the rue Poissonnière that she likes so much now, and that she used to flee from before, as her daughter fled from it also. To build the house was Uncle Maurice's idea, the brother of her great-grandmother, a retired colonel, on waste-land next to the Prévost Chocolate Works, Proust's favourite, on the boulevard side.

Now her house is in the heart of the Sentier district. Taxi drivers don't like going there. 'It's not my fault if you live in a grotty area'. She loves the district she lives in. This street has become a sea of knitwear. When she was young, she could do her shopping at the Italian's on the way home from the office.

She swims. She's no longer cold now. This tingling sensation reminds her of the tingling sensation at Biarritz when her daughter was eighteen months old and she was spending her last holidays in the Basque country with her great-grandmother.

– Tell me a story, mummy.

Incapable. She should have been worried on account of the entry on her passport: 'Writer'. She thought: 'A writer isn't a story teller. It doesn't matter if I can't tell stories.' Yet she thought she knew well enough *Cinderella, Tom Thumb, Queen Mab's Twelve Daughters, The Little Matchgirl, Joan of Arc, Napoleon, Blue Beard.* But when it came to telling them, there was always a blockage, the same inability as with her book today. It should have put her on her guard.

She didn't know, when she was teaching her daughter to swim at Biarritz, when she was so young that she was oblivious to her youth, that she would one day find herself in the Breton sea, somewhat solitary, regenerating herself, so as to be able to return to the others, those others whom she loves and cannot do without.

She loves the others so much that, since she has been sleeping alone, she falls asleep listening to music. It keeps her company. When she wakes up, she hears voices. The other night, it was a woman expressing surprise: 'You are my first anaesthetist! That's two firsts this week. A lawyer's clerk and an anaesthetist.' A woman fades away into the night and the young woman goes back to sleep. If that woman has an anaesthetist and a lawyer's clerk, what have I got?

IX

She has the old gentleman waiting for her on the beach with a large white towel.

– I mustn't let him bug me, mutters the young woman to herself. I haven't been abandoned by my loved ones just to have an old man looking like Clemenceau latch on to me.

He looks at her as if she were good enough to eat.

– Women can stand cold water better than men.

– It's because I'm plump.

– You're plump. . . but firm.

That's it. He's won her over. He has just told her exactly what she wanted to hear. She is firm, she is solid. Her parents endowed her with health. She will come back strong and able to make a fuss of them.

– Get dressed quickly. You could suddenly get cold.

The young woman gets undressed in the hut.

– He's not going to tell me what to do, this old codger. I must be on the look out and keep my independence.

Keep it? What for? How silly she is. Here she is, alone in Roscoff and she wants to fend him off.

Moreover she isn't any good at fending people off. She has always fended people off very badly. She has never been any good at fending for others either, protecting them from themselves. She had no sense of values, neither a sense of evil nor a sense of sin.

It was doubtless her lack of a sense of sin that led her – in all her guilelessness – to like complicated (difficult) people. Her heart went out to pariahs. She had only ever loved sexual pariahs. In what some people call deviance she had always seen real suffering. Sometimes she loved them before they knew themselves who they were. As she lacked confidence in herself to the point of being comic, other people's difficulties scuppered her. This was perhaps one of the clues to the muddle she was in, but she was proud of loving those she loved.

There, in that hut, on her first day in Brittany, she awarded herself a diploma for having loved difficult people. It was not like Clemenceau's yachting. If she had quite simply been naive, she had to admit that it was too late to do anything about it now.

He was weeping warm tears on her shoulder. 'I can only go to bed with prostitutes.' 'Well, you can go to bed with me then, I am a prostitute.' She thought that that was the finest way to force his love: to convince him that she was one. All women dream about being prostitutes, if being a prostitute means knowing how to love.

Not knowing how to go through the motions of love, but being capable of love. Because love exists, it is devastating, elusive, eternal, but it does exist. It begins with a racing heart, eyes lowered and there it stops. Then comes what is known as love play, and all too quickly you don't know what the other person is feeling and all of a sudden you don't know much about yourself either, but when, like the young

34

woman at Roscoff, one comes to take stock - as they say -
you can recognize love a mile off.

To find him again now, she'd have to look at a map; Aleppo,
Damascus, Ghardaïa, Tangier, Istanbul, Palmyra, Amman.
But she had understood his way perfectly, and when she
made her friends laugh by saying: 'He has found a sexual
solution to his political problems', she knew exactly what she
meant, and as she had had to come to terms with her
suffering, she had decided that she would suffer according to
her own standards and that, if he had loved awful middle-
class people, it was then that she would have been ashamed.
    What's more, all things considered, each time she had
'flared up', she had preferred to have a good opinion of her
rivals, male or female, rather than the contrary.
    - I recommend The Talabardon for lunch.
    My word, the young woman thinks, he takes himself for
the Minister for Leisure.
    - But you see I'm on half board at the Arcades.
    - The best restaurant in Roscoff was The Lobster in Love
but the chef died two years ago and I don't know who has
taken over.

X

In the dining room at the Arcades, the young woman sucks at cool crab claws. Did the old gentleman have to bother her with a dead cook whom she didn't even know? She has enough dead people as it is. Indeed, even if her suffering is apparently attributable to the living, she has all these dead people cluttering up her mind. There are those who died of natural causes and those who died of unnatural causes. A's suicide when he was twenty-five. He hadn't had time to do anything. A. was the first young Arab she had known. He was a tightrope-walker. He killed himself – as they say – after falling from the wire and realizing that he would no longer be able to do the only job he knew. He killed himself also – she remembers – because he didn't know how to write properly and felt vulnerable faced with the world as it is. He killed himself because he ached all over. She remembers his look, radiating tenderness, gentleness whenever he passed by the door on the rue Poissonnière. In her hot-headedness of those days, she had not recognized the signs of imminent death. Every day when she tries to write, her eyes light on that childish face as it was when he worked in the circus at the age of eight. There is also the death of her brother, burnt

36

alive in a fire with his two little daughters. She doesn't think about that enough. One mustn't think with words. One must let the dead live within one. It's the only way to help them bear the separation. She had been inattentive towards this brother quite simply because at that time she was preoccupied with her work and thought she was indispensable.

She had found it amusing, when she had gone to live in the south after the death of her mother, to meet someone who used to come and see her very often in her office, but who didn't recognize her in the bar at Saint-Tropez: he could only identify her behind her desk. People frequently associate you with your place of work. You see them furrowing their brow and scraping the depths of their memory: 'Where can I have seen her?'

Her friend was dead too, she often thinks about her, especially because she didn't want to die. She knew that she would be replaced very quickly. It's the unbearable image of her coming back, of the face she would pull if she returned to this life, that rends her heart.

They prepared her well on that front. They did not let her down. They needed something else. Other people. One is only the central pivot of another's life through nagging. She doesn't go in for harassment, even with her overflow of love, her need to put things into words.

In her mind she parades all of her own dead people. She goes over them in the dining room of the Arcades.

Here she is at Roscoff invaded by memories of the sun and of dead people. Nonetheless she will, imperceptibly, return to life. She will return to life, deprived of everything she thought it impossible to do without.

37

Here she is alone at Roscoff and in cemeteries scattered through the four corners of France, a France which she will find a little more beautiful each day. Here she is, rising from her own ashes. No, it's not her. Because the young woman at Roscoff was her, thirteen years ago, just after the mirages of 1968. She is going to attempt in this book – in this attempt at a book – to combine the two young women, the one without hope and the one with hope. You can do anything in a book. But she has, latent within her, so many books that she hasn't managed to write, so many stories that have stuck in her throat, that she tells herself that this time, because she is a bit more self-disciplined, a bit more experienced, perhaps she'll manage it.

XI

She had already experienced a blockage in writing with her first book. It was the story of her passion for a homosexual. It was doubtless this love that had ordered (or rather disordered) the course of her life. D. had given her back her manuscript with the words: 'Such a great passion. . . and such a little book. And what's more, it's very badly written.' It was true, she wouldn't write it the same way today. She has perhaps made some progress on that front. To grow old is also to make progress. A wrinkle, progress, rheumatism, progress, a pain, progress.

Between each book – and she really was modest about them, modest on account of other people: her models, her idols, and modest on her own account: her lack of staying power. Between each book, she had always needed several years and something or someone to set her free to write.

Her head was full, her heart was full, her heart empty of all the books she hadn't managed to write.

Without doubt the most ambitious was 'The Journey in Egypt'.

She had thought she would be able to go back to the Arab countries with him. Many women happily travel with their husband's mistress. Many men go about with their wife's lover. But this passion for the Arab world was so strong in him, so overwhelming. It encompassed the land, the music, mint tea, cumin, ras el Hanout, bulgour, Koranic prayer beads. It encompassed also words, those words that she had such difficulty in mouthing.

He loved speaking Arabic with taxi drivers, waiters, the boatmen on the feluccas at Luxor. Won over by a deceptive gentleness, she tried to like them, but she came to an all too brutal realization of the fascinating bisexuality of these men who see no more in a woman than her reproductive loins.

He, the silent one, who in the west forgot to speak, was almost talkative. Arab words came from his throat, harsh, joyful, like pearls from the mouths of princesses in the fairy stories of her own childhood. He liked no other words than these now. He wanted to lead the Spanish language into the Arabian desert. He wanted to take Isabella the Catholic Queen to Mecca. He whose intelligence verged on genius melted like Turkish delight on the soil of Egypt.

– How well your husband speaks Arabic!

She would answer:

– He loves languages.

She wasn't likely to forget the look of the legless cripple who at Karnak was getting about on a little iron three-wheeler and who held out his hand with the words 'Broken, Madame. Cassé!', and the sand on the road leading through the mountains to Deir el-Bahari that still burnt her feet. Tireless Arab children pursued her selling Egyptian statuettes (fakes): Rameses, Anubis, Tutankhamun. She had got them all above the radiators in the rue Poissonnière now. She remembers the wild feeling that filled her when confronted with the perfection of that temple where jealous men had destroyed the image of Queen Hatshepsut.

When she used to go to Arab countries with him, she felt that he was possessed, under a spell. It was as if his lot had been cast for something more powerful than writing, more powerful than sexuality. He was capable of becoming passionately involved in the schooling of the children of his illiterate friends, he who perhaps didn't remember how many children his brothers had.

She couldn't manage to describe Egypt. All her memories of its beauty had received painful blows like the face of the queen. Yet all her images of happiness were linked to the sun, to warmth, to the sea. The first time she saw the Nile, in that ineffable morning light at Luxor, she had thought she would faint at the sight of such purety, a purety that can only be compared to that of the voice of that woman who sings the Lieder of Strauss.

XII

The waiter approaches the young woman and places a dish of mussels on her table.

The young woman gathers up her courage.

– Can you show me the wine list?

The doctor, that doctor she hates, the one who told her: 'I see Brittany as the only solution for you', didn't forbid her to drink wine. What's more, if he had done so, she wouldn't have obeyed him. She likes wine. Her friends make fun of her because she puts ice cubes in it. It's because of a man she believed herself to be very much in love with and who liked chilled wine with ice cubes. Life is strange. She doesn't know if she didn't imagine this love, but twenty years later, the ice cubes are still there.

– Which wine is the lightest?

– It's our Côtes du Rhône.

– I'll have a bottle.

She is going to flaunt her iced Côtes du Rhône under the noses of all her neighbours. She won't be able to put up with Brittany if she doesn't drink wine.

No, she hadn't imagined that love. His name is M. A few days before being sufficiently sad to leave for Roscoff, she had sat down with him quite by chance, in the bistro of their youth. They talked for half an hour. The years were swept away. His voice was the same. So was his face. There was still the same understanding between them. They were in the same bistro. The owners had changed and it had been redecorated. But they were the same, only had led different lives. Not opposite. Not parallel. Different. It was he who said after meeting her husband: 'There's the Spaniard we've been waiting for for years.' In love with M.- who was not free and who did not love her – she had taken that sentence as a command. He had thrust her into the arms of the Spaniard. Thus either directly or indirectly, he had set the course of her life. She owed her husband to him, her pain and her joy. It was also on account of M. that she was in Roscoff. All this loving that is not reciprocated makes you and breaks you. She thought about it without anguish. In truth she was only grieving. She pitied those who had never loved.

It comes back to her that it is rather hard being on one's own. Wine is for sharing. Really everything is for sharing, life, books, films. That is perhaps what is most difficult for her: no longer sharing everything.

She had already had problems with the world of Spain, and now she must try and follow him into the African desert. Even if she does all she can to understand him, this sharing is painful. She knows that sharing is often an illusion among couples and she cannot bear, never has been able to, women who speak in the plural, even when she believed herself to be happy and sharing: 'We loved Muriel', 'We can't stand the Riviera any more', 'I was just saying so to François'. For some women, marriage is a big cake and they only speak with their mouths full. They are a bit mad. One is never

43

inside the other person. The other is always within his own unique absence.

Obviously, drunkards and public personages can become your prisoners. She remembers her friend, so jealous, so betrayed, who used to telephone ten times a day to her husband's secretary. 'I thought he had an appointment at ten thirty.' 'No, Madame, his appointment is at eleven o'clock.' The half hour became for her friend – she had never told her but she knew it – the occasion for the most diabolical adultery. As if, in half an hour between two doors he could experience love. Her friend could not accept this; what she had accepted, for a long time now, but with much difficulty, is that one is never inside the thoughts of the other person.

XIII

The young woman asked too many questions. She was a walking questionnaire when she was younger. A surprising response: they had left, those whom she questions now: the head of the king of Morocco on a letter, with or without his head-dress. On her daughter's letters a Greek church, a Greek peasant woman, the Republic of Italy, the Statue of Liberty, Thomas Jefferson, Eisenhower, a Mexican lizard, a Mexican village (called Guerrero), a 'Medieval sculpture' from India (the India of her emotions), tea plucking, Indian also, an Indian elephant of such gentleness and her daughter was so ruthless at that time. The Taj-Mahal, the Shah of Iran, a fine brightly coloured bird, three Afghan chieftains, a Turkish president, a Peruvian snake, a Greek allegory, a fish from El Salvador, John Fitzgerald Kennedy on a stamp from El Salvador, Queen Elizabeth smiling on a journey to Brazil.

Her daughter had made those journeys with a boy who would have been called a lout in her own family, who was perhaps in reality a lout. He was an orphan from Nice. She had the feeling that her daughter loved him passionately. She realized that with her foolish talk, she had given her a taste for lame ducks. Despite her bad upbringing, with her emotional

45

and political bric-à-brac, she had given her in essence all that she held dear herself. And it wasn't because she had, along with the others, been a party to a kind of shipwrecking of their ideas. That she had changed sides. She would always be on that side. Morally her position was to be never on the winning side. Her daughter was the same as herself, even if in order to grow up, she had had to insult her, bite her on the shoulder in an attempt to wrench her passport away when she was fifteen, to yell out that she wouldn't ever be like her. She thought that her daugher had suffered even more than herself because she had made no compromises with herself. She knew that if she had learned about revolt in her heart and through books, her daughter had lived through it in reality. She still trembled to think of the risks she had taken. It was rather as if her daughter had been to war and she had not. She had stuffed herself with words, her daughter had really got burnt.

If only she had been able to think, as she warmed the feeding bottles in the rue Poissonnière, that one day she would only know about her what she wanted to tell her and that she would be reduced to scrutinizing the faces of foreign heads of state in order to try and understand her.

Her daughter was secretive because the young woman had wanted to be open – open in the sense that she believed you should say everything. She believed in words. She believed so much in forms of words that she was to suffer in her flesh on account of them. She, the talkative one, would have a lot of trouble in expressing herself, but she wants to be cured, and at Roscoff she is going to learn to find again the people she loves. . . and perhaps the words as well.

She is happy to have experienced in her flesh that writing means suffering. The giant of the Mississippi, so small in stature, so great in his writing, had told her so before the birth of her daughter.

'Writing is sweat and tears'. She hadn't wanted to believe it at the time. She thought that words would flow from her pen like the Côtes-du-Rhône flowing down her throat.

She believed in words and she believed in the strength of the love she brought them. She thought she could fix them in her embrace and that the three of them would become the image of a family; strange, perhaps, but indissoluble.

For days on end she looked at photographs of her husband and her daughter in order to try and find out what was behind their eyes.

Her life has been ruled by eyes, his look that is overwhelming when he is emotionally involved, the eyes of her dead mother. The look of her daughter refusing to allow her mother to melt like ice. Her fleeting glance, hiding emotion. Her look that means: 'That's none of your business.'

Now the young woman, the one who is cured, not the other, knows that she was right and she sees her daughter, madly in love, bending over the blue eyes of her grand-daughter, and she too will one day send letters from the ends of the earth.

She is on the brink of tasting what develops into knowledge. You need to be unable to make sense of things, of people in order to be able to discover them ultimately. All in all, she has only ever been afraid of their death. It was after the death of that young Arab and of her own mother that she understood that the real tragedy is the death of the other person, and that it is better to know that the person one loves is alive and with another, male or female, than dead. And it's in that respect – she almost made herself smile – that she

47

found herself rather special. Others preferred the death of the other person. With a sort of secret dignity she has got used to them living outside of herself. For years it was unbearable. She suffered in her flesh when he told her one day that his friend had had an accident at work. 'You can't imagine how beautiful Mohammed was in his plaster cast.' He, the son of wealthy Spaniards, could not penetrate the depths of love – or what passes for love – except in the company of men with hands roughened by the society that produced him. She had suffered in her flesh and then she had found a certain grandeur in it and seen that it was typical of their values.

She remembered one Sunday evening when he had come home after reading a letter to an illiterate Arab in a café near the boulevard Barbès, a letter telling him of the death of one of his children. The Arab had furrowed his brow trying to remember which one of his sons was dead. That evening she had forgiven him everything, she had forgiven herself everything. If it was in order to arrive at that point that he had pursued that path, she understood perfectly.

She had at first been somewhat wounded, as she had been when her first husband had left her, but she sincerely believed that there was a true beauty, hidden away somewhere, and she, who had been so bossy, jealous, possessive, critical, that she rummaged through wastepaper baskets and dustbins in order to try and understand them, had been shattered one day when she came across a huge blue sheet of paper that she had mistaken for a tax return: it was the pay advice of the worker with whom he was in love at that time – her rival – and on this pay advice was written: 'unable to write'.

Now this worker, who had learned to read and write thanks to the literacy classes at the Renault Works, had returned to Morocco. The young woman knew that in the living room of the house he had been able to build over there, he had put up a photo of herself and her husband along side a fine picture of the Mont-Saint-Michel with a thermometer attached to it. This picture was a gift from her husband.

The young woman, who was conscious of the degree of perversity present in a writer who loved only illiterates, was grateful to him for having given her a glimpse of that world.

When she had been expecting her daughter, street sweepers in the gutter of the rue de l'Université had mocked her: 'Who's knocked you up then, doll?' She had laughed, with joyful laughter. If they spoke to her like that, it was because they knew she had made love.

Twenty years later, other workmen, sweeping the same gutter, immigrants with calloused hands, were to become her rivals.

XIV

The young woman searches for sleep. She tosses back and forth in her bed with its rough sheets. She reaches out with her arm to check that he's not there. It's rather a theoretical checking: she has got used to sleeping alone. But she would have quite liked at Roscoff to sleep with some stranger, a heart with no strings attached, someone whose wife had just left him for an Arab worker. They would have spoken the same language. It could have been a pleasure. She would have told him nothing about herself. Yes, perhaps that she was a widow. The first – second – third –? man she had loved used to say that a widow was an erotic object. She would have been this stranger's erotic object. They would have felt very free, being sure of never seeing each other again.

She would have quite liked to turn up at the doctor's and say to him: 'Hello, doctor, I'm better, but I caught V.D. in Brittany. Can I get it seen to on the National Health?' But she can't catch V.D. like catching a fish.

She likes hotel bedrooms. They are places special to happiness and unhappiness alike. They tore each other apart in a room in Venice. In a hotel called the Montecarlo. They tore each other apart before having been able to analyze the depths of their problem. She saw him turn his face to the wall to weep. It was really too much to bear. This imbalance between them, she didn't know that it was due to Africa. He didn't know it either. Afterwards he had a high temperature and they both felt better. She believes in crises. She believes in outbursts. She doesn't believe in bottling things up. She believes in spelling things out. That's also one of the reasons why she is going to try and write that book. So that the others can recognize themselves in it.

– All in all, Madame, yours is a very special case.

– Not especially, doctor.

One Sunday – it always happens on a Sunday because Sunday is the workers' day off – he came home looking very handsome with his face all pure and smooth. He had been to the Turkish baths and then made love with an Algerian. She had been overwhelmed by the beauty (on the moral plane also) that emanated from him on that day. As it is not possible to ask questions on these fringes of indecency she had simply asked him: 'Where were you?' And he had answered: 'At his place.' And as he had seen that she had made progress in understanding and tolerance, he had added: 'When his wife came home, she made us some coffee.' 'His wife?' 'Yes, he's married to a woman from Brittany.' 'Where do they live?' 'Near the Gare du Nord.' 'What does his wife do?' 'She works at the factory.'

Near the Gare du Nord, a Breton working woman was going through the same thing as herself. Not only was she no longer

51

alone but had become universal. The Breton woman was a better person than she. The young woman was very tolerant, but she wouldn't have made them coffee. In the first place, making coffee bores her and secondly, because she has quite enough fanciful images, she has no need of real ones.

All these men, she loves them from the bottom of her heart. She loved them when they were humiliated, oppressed, and here they are, pinching her husband from her. She doesn't want to think wicked thoughts. She must forgive.

But then, there is nothing to forgive. What she was unable to give him, they gave him. He is at peace now; that peace that is relative in writers, but when they had met he had been tottering on the brink of death. He wanted to die because he hadn't come to terms with himself. She was totally incapable of alleviating his pain. At the time when de Gaulle was giving independence to the African nations, the Arabs were giving her husband his independence. She had lived through an historical situation parallel to that of her country. Despite her taste for confidences, it had taken her several years before she had been able to tell people of that path she had trodden. It's like her book, it's like death, things need to be digested before you can talk about them. Despite her charitable thoughts, she was sometimes angry with these Arab men who find every justification for their freedom in the Koran. She had to admit that the Bible – even if one knows it badly – is more of a burden than the Koran.

XV

The young woman still cannot sleep. She gets up and opens the window. The Breton night is beautiful. She breathes in the sea air. Purifying. A purifier. She fills her lungs. She is pregnant with pure air.

She regrets the children she has not had. That was on account of her hotheadedness, the feeling of being indispensable at work, the notion that one hasn't got the time. In the time that she spent waiting for stupid telephone calls, she could have brought up three children. She would have made their bottles, their vegetable broth, taken them for walks, bathed them. It's exhilarating washing a child's body, spreading it with fragrant cream. She would have taken them to the circus. She would have helped them with their homework.

God knows she was in favour of abortion. (God again, why God?) But she missed her children. She missed them because she suddenly said to herself, looking at the sea at Roscoff, that they had been de luxe abortions. She had jealously preserved her liberty and now she found herself alone.

XVI

On the second day, it rained cats and dogs. The young woman sat down at her table and wanted to start writing her book, but alas it was still much too soon.

In the rain, at Roscoff, she wasn't going to be able to conjure up Egypt with a wave of a magic wand. She wouldn't manage to get moving that tiny fairy-tale boat that travelled up the Nile at five kilometres an hour.

She wasn't going to be able to conjure up the wonderful heat, that the others couldn't stand but that she loved to distraction. She wasn't going to be able to rediscover the taste of peanut sauce or of grilled pigeons.

Yet she could see the boat very clearly. She could see the deck, the cabins, the lounge, the dining room. She could see, standing on the quayside at Luxor, the suitcase of the Dean, a clerical gentleman.

For two weeks they had thought that the Dean was having a relationship with a young man who was travelling with him. They were on a package tour, travelling up the Nile with a group. Her husband had forbidden her – she who so much enjoyed talking about her life – to say that they were writers. Actually she wasn't since she couldn't manage to write.

So they had said nothing and Egypt takes possession of one so completely that one can walk on the deck of the Oonas reading *Dox Quixote* or the *Blue Guide* and never talk about oneself.

On the last day of the trip, a young woman with short brown hair admitted that she worked for the Ministry of Education and suggested that everyone now say what they did for a living. The young woman was ecstatic at the thought that she was now able to admit to her fine career. Her husband was furious. The girl from the Ministry began by asking the Dean: 'Are you in banking or the Church?' The Dean stroked his chin, smiled and answered: 'The Church.' The Dean and the young man were priests. Egypt is so absorbing that they had lived for two weeks with two priests, without knowing it, between Cairo and Aswan.

She remembered that in Cairo, when they had been walking around the Ibn Touloun Mosque in the unspeakably poor districts that her husband had always found it easier to bear than herself, with the Dean and his friend, the two men groaned: 'Let's go! Let's go!' 'It's too much! It's too much!'

Then, like tourists from every country in the world, on every journey in the world, they bargained for djellabas, necklaces, slippers.

The young woman loved bargaining. It was her Jewish streak and perhaps her own way of playing with the Arabs. She was very good at it and loved to laugh with them when she had won at bargaining for some mauve, green or pink djellaba for her best friend. There was no vengefulness in her bargaining. Well before she knew he was a homosexual, well before he knew it himself, she enjoyed bargaining.

XVII

Yesterday in a taxi she had been listening to the radio on France Inter or Europe No 1. A doctor was talking about Indian children being sent down the mines at the age of five, about little Japanese of eleven with their long thin fingers making the transistor radios that we buy for a song. The taxi driver got cross: 'Well, Madame, they're not going to ask us for money for that lot. I don't give a damn about them. There are still fifty thousand maharajahs who are million-aires in their country! Let them soak them! It's not our business!'

The young woman replied, lacking courage: 'It is awful, you know, to send such young children out to work.' The taxi driver retorted: 'They ask for money to give to the parents so that they won't send their children out to work. Do you feel like giving any?'

In his taxi on the Place de la Concorde, ready to cry over little Indians, she who drove bargains in Luxor, Benares, Marrakesh and the Carreau du Temple, had to admit that this taxi driver had put his finger on the contradictions inherent in the Left to which she belonged and which had just come to power.

Not her. She hadn't come to power. Because her brand of left-wing politics was gilded and idle. She was not militant. Through egoism? Through idleness? Because she didn't believe in the written word, she who just couldn't? Through cowardice or because she had been horrified by the unbearable lessons given by certain people? Because the failure of socialism on a world scale was too blatant? No, she hadn't been militant because she was lazy (in that domain) and also because she hadn't wanted to fall back into that wonderful collective illusion that makes you forget everything. Perhaps also she hadn't been a militant through lack of generosity, she who believed herself to be so generous.

But she did sell a newspaper on the corner of the rue Poissonière and the rue de Cléry. Her daughter was four years old and loved those Sundays when, crouching on the pavement beside her mother, she would listen to her shouting: 'Buy the. . . Read the. . .'

Then one day the young woman decided that she no longer wanted to (no longer could) sell that web-of-lies-paper and pathway to future miseries: history. She didn't know how to tell her daughter. She told her suddenly: 'We won't be selling the paper any more.' 'Why?' 'Because I don't agree with it any more.'

Her daughter looked at her mother, her eyes full of longing for all the bottles of orangeade the young woman's friends had bought her on Sunday mornings, and she said simply: 'Can't we sell another paper?'

XVIII

The tortuous paths of the writer's craft – the young woman is in her room in order to try and rediscover the palm trees bending over the Nile, Rameses II, Amenophis and Queen Hatshepsut, and she can't find them. She thinks of her friend who was brought up in Egypt, naïve, gentle, monogamous and monolithic, madly in love with her husband, so pure and so simple, breathing in Egypt through every pore of her skin. Halva, hair removing wax perfumed with lemon and honey, rice with pine kernels, the Turkish baths (she as well), the good aroma of spices, figs, hot peppers. There she is walking in the rain with her friend. Her thoughts of her are full of tenderness and yet it was her husband that she loved most.

He had wanted to get to know her after her second book. So the young woman is right, books point the way to everything. It wasn't Egypt that she was looking for at that time, it was the south. And now twenty years later, still thanks to that book, a very gentle yet very violent friendship had been born. A friendship that means that one lives one's life without feeling too much of a stab at the idea that it will have to be given up or that one's own life is off-course. There she is being borne aloft in a boundless lyricism of affection for her dark-skinned Egyptian friend, like a sun-ripened apricot, they have grown old together and she overwhelms her by being madly in love with that man.

Before the window that she has opened in order to breathe in the rain, the wind, the smell of sea-weed, before this window that is shutting out Egypt for her, that is distracting her from writing that book, she finds herself full of this friend who likes Arabs and Jews because she is Jewish and was born in Cairo, this friend who admits to having known nothing before meeting him, and has been content to live her life through him, their son and her own family. The egoism of Jewish women? The egoism of monogamy or a languid, touching morality, leading her to the banks of the Nile, but not the Nile of her book, the Nile of tenderness.

She cannot rediscover that extraordinary light she caught sight of one morning while crossing the Nile at Luxor, but she is thinking about her friend. She realizes that they have their past in common and that they have helped each other to live. She remembers that when she received the letter he wrote to her before their departure for Moscow, the letter in which he had admitted to her everything she had refused to guess at and which shattered her, it was them she had rung. Him, because she always turned to him for support when she was in trouble (it was rather in ordinary things that he was difficult to pin down) and her, because she was tender, good and precisely because she understood nothing of the problems of homosexuality, her understanding would be all the sweeter to her. She had spoken to them in the first place also because she knew that they loved him.

Beneath the rain at Roscoff, she thinks about her life that has got a bit out of control (what an under-statement!) She sees him, walking through a desert she does not know (Tafilalet, Timimoun, Touggourt) and suddenly, horrified at being pleased to see him, she catches sight of the old gentleman trotting along in the rain, wearing a shiny yellow mac, followed by a black dog.

XIX

In a bistro, over a glass of Muscadet, the old gentleman has started to tell her the story of his life. She would never have thought she was ready to hear it.

He had been a radio telegrapher on a ship going to the colonies, the 'San Diego'. He had been married very young to the girl with the white sunshade. She had been unfaithful to him with Armand, his best friend, who had been a witness at their wedding. He had found out at Djibouti, his favourite port of call, from a letter that he suspected came from Armand's wife.

The old man had forgiven. He was thirty at that time, and at every stop in port, especially at Djibouti, he had known real moments of happiness with experienced, smiling negresses.

At the third glass of Muscadet, he admitted to her that he had been so afraid of disappointing his wife, with whom he was so much in love, that he had had too much to drink on his wedding night and had rolled off the bed. She had never really forgiven him (often women just don't want to know about men's traumas).

– I was afraid of her innocence, sighed the old gentleman.

61

Damn those pure young things!

The young woman smiles. People are surely not afraid of innocence any more. She remembers her own fear and especially the fear she had for her daughter. 'You have a serious responsibility' snapped the moralizing paediatrician who could not accept that her daughter had grown up. 'It's not possible for them to get any pleasure. It's all provocation.'

The young woman had lowered her head. She couldn't really see why she should be reassured by the thought of her daughter not getting any pleasure. If she were not getting any pleasure, she would go even further and what did that mean in 1968, going further? The young woman would simply have liked to help her to live, to arm her for life. She looked this nasty doctor straight in the eyes. She hated him, him as well, for having brought her to such a military sounding phrase when thinking of her daughter's love affairs. She could feel only pain if her daughter felt nothing. And suddenly, with a libertine's joy, she hoped with all her might that the doctor, yet again, had made a wrong diagnosis.

Suddenly she sees again her daughter as she was at fifteen, separating her eyelashes with the point of a pin.

– Where did you learn to do that?

– At school, we get so bored.

Then she plunges into the blue eyes of the old gentleman that suddenly scupper her. She is immersed. She is happy. After a litre of Muscadet, he lets her swim. She wonders to which breed that look belongs and if he really sees her. She wonders if he is consciously letting her dream, or if he's simply unaware. She abandons herself to those blue eyes that have become so welcoming.

XX

You were happy on your boat?

– The sea takes more than it gives. One finds one's sea legs, but the heart gets left behind.

– How do you tell one day from the next?

– On Sundays you have drinks in the captain's cabin.

– What about the seagulls?

– I ate them sometimes, when there was nothing else on board, but I didn't enjoy them. They taste of fish.

'If seagulls taste of fish,' thought the young woman, 'then what does my body taste like?'

The old gentleman gives her some winkles that she extracts from their shells with a pin. Then he has another glass of Muscadet.

– She was so sweet when she had just come from Armand. 'You're not hungry are you? You're not thirsty? You've not got too many worries at the moment?'

The young woman remembers the extraordinary tenderness that overcame her when she felt guilty. She looks at the old gentleman.

He is no longer a stranger. She already knows a lot about him. It's all the more amazing as she has just invented him.

He is her prisoner.

Has she just made her début in literature? Will she be able to carry him off to Egypt on her boat? Will she be able to fall in love with him if she can slow down the pace of time? She has given him the blue eyes of the men she has loved. Her daughter's daughter will have blue eyes as well.

She has invented him because she doesn't want to be alone at Roscoff. She is in command. That's what she thinks. Miracles in writing are not always what one expects. This old gentleman, apparently harmless, whom she invented to keep herself company, this stranger who lends her his beach hut, this man who has been deceived by his wife and who has found a kind of peace with Babaoudia, a wonderful negress at Djibouti, is quite capable of making her suffer.

She doesn't want to know about that. She is here to cure herself of other people. If he makes her suffer, that will be a fresh wound. She wants something new.

She will get it. It is quite possible to experience a youthful suffering brought about by a very old man.

XXI

That morning Roscoff was flooded with sunlight. The young woman could hardly believe her eyes. When she got to the beach, the old gentleman was playing 'boules' with men in white whom she took to be the nurses from the Roch Kroum Marine Institute. He had his back to her: he was throwing the boule. He didn't see her coming. She was pleased. She was prepared to accept his bathing hut on account of the wind, his confidences over the Muscadet when it was raining, but was quite determined to keep herself to herself.

The young woman lay down on the sand for a few minutes, keeping her pullover on, her eyes closed. Then she took off her pullover and almost tasted the joys of the south. Children were playing ball above her head. She wondered – perhaps somewhat less anxiously than the previous day – where her daughter was. Then she wondered when she would again lie on a beach with her. She was sure of one thing: she had given her the sea. She had given her a taste for the sea. A love of the sea. Now her daughter knew more seas than she did. She had bathed in the Pacific, in the Indian Ocean. She had even been unfaithful to the sea with Lake Titicaca and perhaps with the Colorado Falls, but this taste for water came from her. One day, perhaps not so far off, they would go back to the beach together. One day she would teach her grand-daughter to swim in the sea. She would dabble about like a duckling. The little girl would say: 'It prickles, it prickles.' Because she would already be able to talk. She would not make with her grand-daughter the same mistakes that she had made with her daughter. It was always truly painful to remember the story of her ineptitude at the Deligny swimming pool where the young woman had spent her springtime lunch hours, waiting for summer, in the company of large families, foreigners, single people, transvestites, sporting types and her daughter.

That spring, her daugher was as flat as a pancake and had enormous eyes. She had red pants on. From the young woman she demanded a bra like hers. The young woman burst out laughing. Her daughter threw a real tantrum. Everyone was looking at them. The young woman, usually so weak, didn't want to give in. She had already given in over the pants. She was so fond of her child's body, naked in the water. She wanted bodies to be able to breathe. She had a whole lot of mental clichés like that about nature. She tried to drag her daughter into the water with her. She howled all the more. A young mother, more perceptive than herself, handed her a strip of material that the young woman tied around the non-existent breasts of her daughter and the child, calm and confident, came and swam with her. She was sure of one thing, she wouldn't do such a stupid thing again.

– Did you sleep well? Despite the rain? But look, it's chased the clouds away. Have you seen how blue the sky is?

– I've seen nothing yet, the young woman replied, but I slept very well.

– It's the sea air. Sometimes it takes a bit of getting used to, the first few days.

*　*　*

– I used to sleep like a babe, but that's gone since my wife died.

Clemenceau is a walking graveyard. Here he is, dragging up the still warm body of his wife. That she does not want. He is on the verge of being indiscreet.

– Is it long since you lost her?

Now it's his turn not to answer. He takes a few steps along the beach and mumbles: 'When I think of her now, I see the young girl with the sunshade.'

XXII

The following night, the young woman had an avalanche of dreams. The worst was one where they made her throw stones at children.

She woke up breathless and in tears, and she thought again of her daughter with passion and violence. They had had to hit her once. Words were no longer having any effect. They couldn't get through. She wasn't listening to them any more. When he had hit her, she had cried out: 'It was about time', as if for years she had been expecting from them the punishment they felt incapable of giving. It had made him weep. Then she had run away, just after lunch. She had disappeared. They were by the sea, in June. Beaches opened up one after the other, like flowers. They had looked for her on all the beaches, on all the rocks, in the woods. She imagined her dead. One always imagines them dead, one's loved ones. It's the wicked who survive. Alive and hard skinned. 'That's all the fault of your upbringing.' Always being accused. Other people reproached her. She was quite prepared to be judged, even burnt, provided she could get her back. They were expecting friends for dinner. Big warm tears fell into the frying pan. She would make them

69

fritters of maternal pain and anguish.

Her daughter had returned towards nine o'clock, her hair in a mess and her arms full of gorse. She had been walking in the mountains. The big departure had obviously been put off until later. She smiled as she asked the adults, who couldn't get their breath: 'What's to eat this evening?' Then she took the gorse off to her bedroom which overlooked the harbour.

The young woman murmured the name of her daughter, then she fell asleep again, this time to meet a Russian doctor whom she did not know. This dream doctor was tall and handsome. He told her that he had never imagined he would meet anyone as wonderful as her. She was taken aback, flattered, happy. All the same, she woke up before anything had happened between them.

She told herself then that if she were starting to dream about people she didn't know, it must mean that she wanted to live.

Then she dreamed about him, it was very curious. He was wearing a tie, he who hardly ever wore a tie. He held her close to him. They were in Africa. A strange Africa that was like the Alsace of her forefathers.

Afterwards she began to sing a German melody possibly from Mahler's *Kindertoten Lieder,* and the music turned imperceptibly into flamenco, then into an Arab song.

He was telling her: 'You can do anything, I love you.'

Day broke and the young woman, an international singer, had won back her wandering husband.

Then she dreamt of the old gentleman who was passion-

70

ately shaking her hands.

When she woke up, it was her own two hands that were clutched to her heart. She didn't feel lonely but filled with great gentleness.

XXIII

After her night of dreams, the young woman got up good-humoured, almost reconciled to Brittany, and she set off for the beach.

She was no longer indignant that the sea was so far out. She walked bare footed on the wet sand. She bent down to pick up green moss and she squashed fresh algae between her fingers.

She didn't know that one could have that kind of relationship with the sea. Running after it. Before it had been people that she had run after. Now she would have to tackle nature, writing, words, if she could ever manage it. She would have to take on the wind, wear clothes to bathe. A whole new morality, new rituals. She was ready for anything.

The young woman was walking in a kind of windy desert. Gauguin's colours, but without the orange and yellow. She had put on a sand-coloured jacket as if to blend with the landscape. Suddenly she felt like sitting down. She found a rock, took off her jacket, looked for a pebble to stop it blowing away. The seagulls were waddling on the sand like ducks. She had trouble finding a pebble.

– You've come at a good time. It's the season for high tides.

She recognized his voice immediately. Emerging from the desert like a Jack-in-the-box, the old gentleman came up to her. He had a butterfly net and a bucket. His dog was following him, bounding.

– I'm going to collect mussels. Are you interested?

– No thanks. I'll stay here.

– Be careful. The sea comes up more quickly than you think. You might be taken by surprise.

He is annoying her. She wishes he would forget her.

The Breton desert is like the African desert. She has seen him move away as the old gentleman is moving away now, becoming no more than a tiny speck in the distance. He got away from her – as they say – but had she ever held him? No, the one she thought she held was not him, as he did not yet know who he was.

She remembers Aubervilliers where they used to go and eat paella with Spanish workers. She remembers José who sang flamenco in the corridor of the train bringing them back from Barcelona to Paris. 'You see,' he told her, 'they take their country with them, on the soles of their shoes.' She didn't know at the time, he hadn't known either, when they were wandering around the port area of Barcelona, drinking Manzanilla and Sherry at the Varadero, she didn't know how far he would go, how far she would have to go in order to understand him.

The last card she had received from him was from Istanbul. The Blue Mosque or Santa Sophia. She had never been there. They had both been there. Suddenly she sees again the mosque of Ibn Touloun in Cairo, serenely

73

luminous. She had sat down on a warm stone, overcome by such beauty. Then she had gone up with him to the top of the minaret and in horror had seen a land of poverty and rags.

Here she is again in Egypt, incapable of describing it. She hears the muezzin calling a whole people to prayer. She hears Oum Kalsoum, and suddenly she can no longer tell whether she can hear *him*.

When he says to her 'I'm going off on a trip' she can tell that he is thinking about those men but also about his work. She experiences the same emotion when confronted with his somewhat crazed look if she interrupts him while he is writing. He is also possessed by writing. After all, there is really nothing to shock her in all that.

His crazed look, she knows it well. Sometimes she is still capable of making him jealous.

– Would you be hurt if I were in love with someone else?

– Undoubtedly if it meant you had a relationship with him as you have with me.

– How stupid he is! She is not likely to come across another Spaniard who reads the Koran, who always has an Arabic grammar book on his bedside table, who goes off at the same time every Sunday to the Turkish baths, who likes harira and who writes fine books that become more and more difficult for other people and for her.

When he didn't know who he was, his language was clear. Then as he moves more deeply into his own lucidity, his books become sybilline. Significant also for a few educated Arabs. Not of course those men whom he meets on Sundays.

– It's the best part of him that makes me suffer.

– You should be happy, says the old gentleman, not to be suffering for something frivolous.

XXIV

The old gentleman becomes intrusive. He should leave her alone a bit to get on with her own sorrow.

So, she didn't say pain. Perhaps she is healing. Formerly she thought that depressions were crises of self-satisfaction. She wouldn't say the same today. It's the body that lets go or is dropped and it's the soul that takes a beating.

She had so brutally lost the little confidence she had in her femininity. Very young, she had seen herself as a woman in memory only. Perhaps at the very moment when her daughter had started to live. She had thought it was her fault that she was living prematurely.

Her fault or not, she had known self-rejection. Now on the road to recovery, she didn't find it tragic, but at the time she had thought that part of her life had been wrenched away from her.

Yet at the beginning, remembering her own naivety, she had sincerely believed that it was better for her daughter to experience life earlier. The young woman could still see the flamboyant mass of hair of a young red-headed girl called Jacqueline Souhaité at Saigon, flirting with a boy, also a red-head, called Yvon Gache. When the two of them walked arm in arm on the boulevard Norodom, and the sun shone through their hair, their wild mingled manes seemed to her the very image of happiness. Of a happiness that would always be forbidden to her. She thought she would be undesirable to the end of her days. All women made her think of sin, and she envied them. Her soul was free, but she didn't know what to do with her liberty. But these two redheads in the sunshine, light against light, she was convinced that they held a secret.

She looks at the sea that has gone far out. She always likes to make the sea a point of reference. That comes from her childhood in Indo-China. She sees again the signboards on Nha Trang beach. 'Beware of sharks'. Life has gone far out from her. Yet she is still alive: it's a difficult patch. Her strength is intact and unused. No one needs her any more. She finds herself in a void.

The doctor had questioned her about her background. Her past no longer needed her. She had lost her surroundings. Her surroundings had left her. All she could do was to wait for them.

Yes, the pain – well, the word was coming back – was that no one needed her any more and she couldn't manage to express that pain and turn it into a book.

XXV

She doesn't even know if she is capable of speaking about the death of her cat. The young woman remembers Mao and bursts into tears. She had had a very ugly cat whom she had loved madly. She had wanted a cat after having seen Malraux on television with a cat on his lap. The following day a friend rang to ask her if she would like a cat. The brother of this friend and her sister-in-law had seen three tiny abandoned cats on the road in Brittany on the way to mass. They had taken a vow (God is everywhere) to bring the three cats back to Paris if they found them still in the same spot on the way back from mass. That is how God decided it. The young woman saw the hand of fate in it. She could not bring herself to go as high as God when thinking of Mao, but she had gone to fetch him with her daughter the day that Che died, and they called him Mao. Actually she had wished for this cat in the most violent phase of her daughter's revolt in order to arouse maternal feelings in her. Her daughter maintained that it was her own maternal problem that she had sought to solve by adopting Mao at the very moment when her daughter was moving out of her control.

The young woman brought Mao up very badly. As badly as she had brought up her daughter, that is to say, without hard and fast rules, without discipline. One day Mao fell from a neighbour's arms. Thereafter he had a gait resembling that of the Buddha and an exaggerated wariness toward human beings. He was the epitome of an unlovely cat.

Desgraciado. She had him for twelve years. There was – as for all people who have animals – the problem of holidays. Who will feed Mao? Who will look after Mao? He was so wild that there was no question of taking him along. Just before her own operation, he was ill and the young nurse who came to give Mao injections said to her one morning: 'You don't look too good yourself!'

Then her husband got asthma. They found that he was allergic to feather pillows and to Mao. So she tried to break with Mao and give him to an old lady who lived in the rue Tiquetonne not far from her own house, and who was in despair because she had just lost her cat. She took him, broken hearted, in a large bag. That same evening the old lady rang begging her to come and take Mao back; he was refusing to eat and wouldn't let anyone near him.

In triumph the young woman brought Mao back to the rue Poissonnière that very evening. He never made a show of emotion. He simply rubbed himself against her legs and purred while he ate.

He walked round the flat as if he were king.

The young woman wrote a letter to her husband – he was in Tangier that year – to tell him that Mao had won. Won. Against whom?

'You are away all the time, but Mao never leaves.'

79

But the following summer, Mao crossed to the other side. Perhaps he had eaten too many sardines, perhaps he was too old, but in any case the vet, who was quite aware of the irrational love the young woman had for her cat, told her that this time there was no more hope, that he was going to be in pain and that he had to be put down.

Her husband came with her to the vet's in the rue Réaumur. The vet told her that the injections were very gentle these days and that he wouldn't feel anything. She told him: 'I want him to die on my lap.' Then the vet said: 'You know it takes at least half an hour.' She replied: 'I owe him that half hour for the sake of all eternity.' She saw him give the injection of death with great delicacy. Then she went and sat in a corner amongst young dogs that were yapping and cats that were miaowing, with Mao on her lap. Her husband, who was sitting next to her, asked her after ten minutes: 'What are we waiting for now?' He hadn't seen the vet give Mao the injection. Sobbing she answered: 'We're waiting for Mao's death.' Her burning tears fell on to the body of Mao which was gradually becoming cold. The vet asked her: 'Do you want another one?' She answered: 'Never.'

When she thinks about it, she still aches all over. Mao – black, wild, Mao – the unforgettable. Mao who was so ugly that everyone made fun of him. Mao who was too fat because she gave him too much to eat. Mao who never gave the least sign of affection. Mao whom children weren't allowed to stroke because he bit. And yet Mao had his place in her heart for all eternity. Mao who is irreplaceable and who belongs to her. Mao will leave her no more.

The young woman realizes that it is now two years since

Mao left her. That young woman is today's young woman – the one who is facing up to life again, the one who believes in life – and yet she never puts her key in the door in the rue Poissonnière without thinking that Mao is no longer there.

And when she leaves the door open to go to the dustbin or to her daughter's or the neighbour's, each time she remembers that there is no longer the risk of Mao escaping down the stairs, and her heart tightens as if she were wearing a bronze girdle.

XXVI

Today is Sunday. The bells ring in a different way. When the young woman opens her shutters, she sees a market by the harbour. She has always loved markets. She gets dressed quickly and rushes down the stairs of the Hôtel des Arcades.

Arab children are playing ball by the harbour. Seeing the onions, carrots and artichokes she remembers that she has no house at Roscoff and that she has undoubtedly not recovered sufficiently to take vegetables back to the rue Poissonnière.

There are black men selling the same necklaces as on the boulevards. A Moroccan tries to sell her a carpet. The market at Roscoff takes her back to the Sentier district and the young woman tells herself that she would be happy if she could write a song of love for the rue Poissonnière. Perhaps her book is neither about Egypt nor the Valley of the Kings but the history of her street.

She deeply loves the house built by her family at the time of the rise of the Nazis in Germany.

It was on her return from Indo-China after the Liberation that she landed in the rue Poissonnière. The caretaker, Mme Renaud, had embroidered the flounces of her crib twenty years previously, at the time when the family was in its heyday. Her husband was an upholsterer. Their daughter slept with Germans and then married an American, but it was thanks to them and the manager Mr Schlesser that the block of flats, owned by Jews, had been spared during the war.

The young woman had at first hated the house as her daughter was to hate it and as perhaps her grand-daughter will hate it later on.

At that time, she thought only of travel, of going away, leaving, like her daughter, like him; but by dint of making herself at home there, she realized that this house, which was less than thirteen years old in 1945 when she arrived there, was her passion and her roots.

She has lived in the rue Poissonnière for more than thirty years now. There are ten or so tenants whom she has known since the Liberation, who have seen her grow old, who have seen her daughter grow up, who congratulated her yesterday on her grand-daughter. She has seen some die and others leave for the country. She and her daughter have occupied the flats of several deceased persons. That of the Chukri Filmers, Turks who faded away one after the other within the space of a few months like two candles and who owned a cherry red crushed velvet armchair, a rococo dressing table, an Astrakhan coat and two silver foxes. They also owned a cinema, 'The Bosphorus'. Monsieur Grison was a drinks salesman. Monsieur Flippo sold buttons. There have been, in this house of her heart, hairdressers, the nurse who had looked after her mother, waiters, a kept woman who owned a lingerie shop, a barrister, a lazy jockey, a colonel, a general, several people who had returned from deportation after the war, of whom one was a dentist, cinema usherettes, a singing teacher, a militant Maoist, the children of a communist leader who left the flat on the pretext that there was a ghost in it, a man who sold carpets, another who sold dates; retired publicans, a representative for Pernod, a milliner, a mirror silverer, a florist, a baker, a watchmaker, a cashier, the niece of a commissioner of police, a greengrocer, an interior designer, a civil servant from the Assemblée Nationale, a journalist, a lorry driver.

And especially there is the indescribable Madame Adèle who does the cleaning for nineteen flats in the block and wears around her waist a bunch of keys worthy of a prison warder. Madame Adèle who tells you at least once a year: 'I'm not so bright this morning, I'm going to my employer's funeral.' Madame Adèle who hides her money under the lino and who lends it regularly to her former employers who never pay her back. Madame Adèle who brandishes in triumph, as if they were love letters, all her IOUs, which of course have no legal value.

Madame Fregoli, the widow of a boxer, who borrowed a million (old francs) from her, invites her to lunch in a sumptuous restaurant. Madame Adèle thinks it is to pay her back and buys Madame Fregoli a bunch of red gladioli. 'We'll have Champagne, my little Adèle', says Madame Fregoli, 'because I'm unable to pay you back; but if you lend me another lot straight away, then we could become associates and open a restaurant.'

'Madame is very kind,' replies madame Adèle,' but I prefer to stay at No 33, I've got used to it.'

The young woman doesn't like to think of the rue Poissonnière as something she's got used to. She loves it too much. She knows the noise of the lift, even its whistling noise when it grates, she knows the noise of the doors that slam to.

The rue Poissonnière is her kingdom, her republic.

It is in the rue Poissonnière that she has been happy and unhappy with her two husbands. It was from the rue Poissonnière that she left with her mother the day her daughter was born. She remembers that her first husband was taking an exam that morning. He had come to see her at midday: she was in the first stages of labour.

Her daughter had been born at five o'clock in the afternoon. They had anaesthetized her for the birth itself, and she still remembers going up in the lift on the way back from the labour ward and hearing the nurse say: 'A lovely little girl. A lovely little girl.'

Twenty eight years later, still in the rue Poissonnière, it would be she who would go with her daughter to another hospital. She was happy to go with her, as her mother had gone with her. Then all three of them had returned to the rue Poissonnière. Her daughter's daughter still holds on to the furniture, but perhaps in twenty years' time, she will be taking her own daughter to the hospital.

In front of the door of No 33, sitting on cardboard boxes emptied of their hundreds of pullovers, there used to be until last year an amazing tramp who would gladly engage in metaphysical discussions. They called him Don Quixote. He was of proud bearing and claimed to be the brother of the mayor of Colmar.

In the rue de la Lune, just opposite No 33, there was also a woman who kept a grocer's shop that sold rotten avocados and who was called Madame Hédiard. Michel Simon used to come and buy potatoes and milk from her. She would indiscriminately suck up to policemen or dustmen who came out of the shop beaming, with a bottle of wine under their arm. She would tell whoever would listen that she knew people in high places, but it didn't stop her being evicted for not paying her rent.

The young woman met her sometimes, a cigarette hanging from her lips. She also had the Sentier district under her skin.

At the seaside at Roscoff, at the dawn of a new love, the young woman dreams of taking the old gentleman off to the rue Poissonnière.

XXVII

The young woman likes Roscoff market. They also sell fish, lace, biscuits and old-fashioned sausage.

There is also a man selling fencing, who has written up on a blackboard 'Free Estimates for Fencing'.

She wonders if she would like to be a prisoner. The prison of her heart is the rue Poissonnière, especially if they return there.

'Whatever you do, don't tell people you live round here,' a man had said to one of her friends who lives in the Sentier district. She had never caught on to the idea of a posh district. She didn't like the 16th arrondissement or the 17th, she felt at ease in districts with no particular identity. 'You don't see a single French person round here any more' said the young woman who waxes her legs in the rue de l'Abbé-Groult.

In the Place du Caire Pakistani men are selling their labour. In the young woman's district, the poor are exploited by those who used to be poor. There is a rotation in poverty. Some – always the same ones – fall on their feet. Others groan in Spanish, Cambodian, Portuguese, Arabic: 'They take all the best places.' As if the Place du Caire were a good place.

The Place du Caire between the rue du Nil and the rue d'Alexandrie, perhaps that's the Egypt she should be talking about. Three sphinxes' heads dominate the entrance to the Passage du Caire. Egypt is everywhere in the Sentier district. The Sentier was originally a path where a starving wolf had appeared in 1613. The rue du Sentier where Mozart's mother died in the early summer of 1778. The rue Poissonnière is also known as the Valley of the Frogs and fish used to be brought by horses from the ports of the Pas-de-Calais. The rue Poissonnière is also the road to the sea.

The young woman likes to hear – as if it were the echo of all her tenderness, all her secrets – the echo of her heels on the pavements of the Sentier district.

Paris is the city of her heart. She is always happy to leave it but she also likes to come back to it. Soon Roscoff will give her the strength to return to Paris.

She hasn't met the old gentleman at the market. It's strange. It is his habit to be always there. Could he be losing interest in her? It would be premature.

XXVIII

Healing implies also a certain amount of ritual. The young woman takes pleasure in her hidden life at Roscoff. She is as if anonymous, incognito, except for the old gentleman, and she hasn't said much to him.

She drinks her tea in bed in the mornings, listening to the news on a little radio that she always has with her. She remembers the day when she was going to work near the Luxembourg and the newsflash she heard in her car at nine o'clock in the morning telling her that the body of the Prince de Broglie was lying in a pool of blood outside No 2 rue des Dardanelles. The body of the Prince de Broglie was for a few seconds still hers, along with those few French people listening to the news at nine o'clock in the morning.

At Roscoff, after listening to the news, she goes and sits in a café and has coffee. In the café, she pretends to be writing, or rather she tries to write in exercise books with squared paper and spiral backs. Madame Amandine, the proprietress, brings her a strong coffee. But, as there is still a blockage, she just notes down all that is being said in the café. She sincerely believes that these little phrases gathered here and there will lead her somewhere. She shouldn't write them letters that would talk of a sadness that might no longer exist when they receive them. It's better for her to try and write that book (which one?) that one day each of them will have on their bedside table with all the words of love she will be able to muster at that time.

She hears a fisherman saying: 'If I didn't do a bit of waitering in the spring, I wouldn't make ends meet.' Then the cleaning woman sighs: 'I dreamt about woods, that means a quarrel.' A woman who works in the market arrives with her dog. She looks at the young woman and says very loudly so that she can hear: 'If only I could write down everything that's going on in my little Mirza's head!' And then suddenly she overhears a conversation about the old gentleman. She doesn't identify him straight away, but as she notes down a few phrases at random she recognizes him: Madame Agatha had run off with Armand.

Madame Amandine wonders if it wasn't he who sunk the boat that drowned them, she and Armand, a few years later. People had thought that he was in Djibouti, but someone had seen him that week in St-Pol-de-Léon.

The young woman likes to think that she is on the brink of loving a murderer. She is pleased that beneath his harmless appearance he conceals so much violence.

The café slowly empties. She is alone with her dusky pink exercise book. It is too early to go off to the beach hut and stretch out on the sand that she is starting to like on his account. She doesn't want to stay in the café doing nothing.

90

To give grounds for talk, however innocent. So she tries to remember all the phrases she has heard up until now in Roscoff and that she wants to put in a book. She can't find any and it's one of his phrases that makes her heart thump: 'Only you can help me to live', and she thinks about the splendid yet heart-rending letter in which he had summed up their life. He didn't know when he wrote to her: 'It's up to you to decide', that eighteen years later they would still be madly in love and not only because their love was impossible.

How strange it is that he is always there to prevent her from falling in love! What an encumbrance an absent husband is! Even his anger turns to abstraction. When she is making soup for him in the rue Poissonnière or he is making her listen for hours on end to Berber flute music or the initiation rites of the whirling dervishes of Konya, she gets angry, but at Roscoff faced with her blank page, she wants to write to him: 'I love you. Yo te quiero.'

XXIX

The young woman has mastered Roscoff now, or rather it's Roscoff that has mastered her. She walks round the village, knowing it now by heart, but her heart is no longer heavy, she doesn't really know why. It is as if a gentle gaiety has come over her, as sometimes one is overcome by a gentle sadness. She is walking in a blue fog, even yesterday it was still grey. She has bought herself a navy blue outfit as if wishing to renew her skin. She goes to the newsagents on the place de l'Eglise. Today she can face the troubles of the world. She likes this village. The doctor was right. She will come back here with him. She will come back here with her daughter, with her grand-daughter, to improve her health after her winter colds. She will take her grand-daughter to the Roch-Kroum aquarium, she will show her the fishes, she will teach her the names of the fishes, the names of the Breton villages. All those names beginning with Ker. Ker means house. The fortunate thing for the young woman is that she likes her house in the rue Poissonnière so much. Perhaps she shouldn't write about Egypt but about the rue Poissonnière. But she will only go back to the rue Poissonnière when she's better, only when she's ready to live again, without them, with them. Certainly without Mao, certainly without the young Arab boy, certainly without her mother. The dead won't return. Clemenceau's Agatha won't return either. That's what they have in common, their dead and the bathing hut. She is looking forward to going there today. She will have a closer look at the photographs. Perhaps she will try and understand who Clemenceau is. He gave her his beach hut on her first day. It was doubless a great stroke of luck for him to lend his hut to an attractive woman. But no, she is not attractive. To a woman then. His advantage over her was that he knew Roscoff and that he owned a beach hut there. Her advantage over him is that he knows nothing about her. So he knows nothing of her unhappiness – which he would undoubtedly not call unhappiness – of her difficulties. Today she is ready for a change of vocabulary.

Suddenly, on the street corner, in the middle of the avenue Victor-Hugo – what's Victor Hugo doing in Roscoff? – she notices a young woman laughing loudly, a young blonde woman, radiant. And Clemenceau, with his back to her – and this time she is furious that he has his back to her – Clemenceau who seems very happy. His back is happy. Clemenceau has a very jolly back. In outline she finds him very young looking. This young man is being unfaithful to her with a blonde. The young woman's heart is racing. Jealous of Clemenceau! That's the limit.

XXX

The young woman has slammed the door of the bathing hut. It makes a funny noise. She feels ridiculous. She is in a very bad mood.

The old gentleman comes up. He was on the beach already.

– I know. It doesn't close very well. Agatha was telling me. . .

– Agatha was telling you! Agatha was telling you! It wasn't Agatha you were chatting to on the avenue Victor-Hugo this morning.

– I was with Madame Olive, the florist. A charming woman.

– Olive is a funny name for a flower seller.

– Her name was Candy before she was married.

– That's even more idiotic.

– Goodness! People's names aren't their fault.

– It only takes a bit of courage to change it.

– Changing a name is very expensive. Flowers don't bring in much money, you know.

– There's no point in flowers at the seaside.

– It's obvious you haven't been to sea! Agatha loved

94

flowers. I loved her way of loving flowers.

The young woman has tears in her eyes. She can't hold them back. She thinks of Mélisande singing with her crystal voice: 'I am not happy here.'

– You're still very delicate, says the old gentleman.

– Have you known Madame Olive for long?

– I knew her when she was a little girl. She used to go to school with Marie.

– Marie?

– Marie was our daughter.

– Was?

– She married a Japanese. She lives in Tokyo now.

– Do you miss her?

– It seems strange. Agatha dead. Marie in Tokyo.

He always brings me back to zero, thinks the young woman, death or absences, but he doesn't annoy me as much as he used to.

XXXI

In the rue Poissonnière there is a photo of her husband that sets her dreaming. It is a photo of him at a Jesuit school in Spain. He has almost the face of a child martyr, his arms folded, eyes lowered, taken in front of a map of the Mediterranean. His left shoulder hides the M of Mediterranean. If the head of his family had known then in what manner he was to cross the Mediterranean! His ancestors had not held back from crossing the seas (the Atlantic and the Caribbean). They had become slave traders in Cuba. That's how they had made their fortune. He had black cousins (sons of former slaves) who had the same name as himself. That's what he was doing penance for. Is love a penance? That's why he had wanted to become stateless. No, perhaps simply because he couldn't stay put in one place. There are wandering Jews pursued by history. There could well be wandering Spaniards pursued by their own life story.

But today she wants to forget him. Let him leave her alone to love in Roscoff this blue-eyed man who doesn't even see her.

XXXII

After the meeting with Madame Olive the young woman had a wild dream. She was walking in a town she didn't know (perhaps Lisbon) and she was looking for the old gentleman. She couldn't manage to get rid of a very boring woman friend who was the only person who knew where he lived because she lived in the same block.

The entrance was straight off the street. On waking the young woman realized that it was the entrance to their house in Spain, but the room where she found the old gentleman was like the cabin of a boat. He was with a girl from one of the Eastern bloc countries. The young woman knew that the old gentleman owed it to her to be nice to her and that she wasn't Polish.

She begged her boring friend to leave. Her friend said to her: 'How can you love a man like that?', and the little Portuguese maid whom the young woman had not yet seen started to cry and said: 'He'll be ruined here.'

Then the young woman saw all four of them eating a very rare steak of which they did not offer her any. So she simply said: 'I'll go and get myself some ice cubes.'

97

Then she found herself alone face to face with the old gentleman. He seemed glad she was there. He whispered gently: 'Would you like to eat a few very fresh oysters with me?'.

XXXIII

That's it, the young woman is caught in the snares of love. She has had to become a grand-mother – a young grand-mother – to discover that she could love an old man. She has had to come wounded to a village full of old people to find herself – young on the one hand and a future old lady on the other.

Everything is possible if one comes to terms with oneself. The young woman hadn't come to terms with herself. She didn't know it. At fifty one ends up getting used to what one is. There are those things one has been able to change and all the other things. What other things? Those notoriously impossible things. Character. The body which doesn't get any better, but which one starts to get to know better. Work. Music. Books one has read. Fatigue. Wrinkles. Renunci-ation.

This is the parcel of life that she is bringing to Clemenceau. This parcel of life that he was not expecting. She mustn't rush him. She mustn't make with him the mistakes she has been making all her life: throwing herself at people like a bull at a gate. She frightened everybody. Her friends. Her lovers. (So she has had lovers.) Her daughter.

To have a lover, one must have been loved. Has she been loved? What is love? She will ask Clemenceau.

This beach hut, it's the Palace he is offering her. It's the Xanadu Palace from *Citizen Kane*. The young woman will sing for the old gentleman.

> *The cicada sang all summer through,*
> *And found herself without reserve*
> *When then the autumn's chill wind blew.*

How is it that one remembers by heart one's first recitation and that one doesn't at all remember the first fluttering of one's heart?

What is the function of memory? What does it cling to? What does it give you in return?

That awful doctor has made her a present of her last love in Roscoff. She will return to the rue Poissonnière having loved an old sailor. She will return to the rue Poissonnière having been loved by a man who no longer expected anything from life. She will return to the rue Poissonnière with a secret that she will tell to no one. She will write a book called: 'I found love at Roscoff.' She will advance so far in her discoveries of love among the senior citizens that her book will become a best seller. It will be known as the geriatrician's Bible. The agelessness of love. A girl at fifty. An Egyptian woman at Roscoff. About love.

The young woman will be the last love of the old gentleman. She will give him that untold happiness. Of forgetting that he is old. She herself, her body against his, will forget her own imperfections. If he can no longer desire her, he will caress her in ecstasy. He will tell her: 'You are beautiful, your skin is soft.' He has already told her that she is firm. 'Plump and firm.' She likes the old gentleman. He is quite surprising. It's because she was seeing only herself that she hasn't noticed.

- I'd like to go to Batz Island.
- It's not very big you know.
- I'd like to take a boat with you.
- Dress warmly. There's a lot of wind sometimes.

XXXIV

The young woman has fallen in love with the old gentleman's voice. Smiling she reflects that he "modulates" well. She likes the verb to modulate. She wonders how he, who is so thin, can manage such fabulous intonations. She has always liked voices, accents. Her husband has a very marked accent. He articulates badly. She adores his voice. She also likes the sing-song voice of her Russian friend. As for herself, she sometimes massacres foreign words in order to reach the other person more quickly. She remembers a play by André Obey that she acted in with her friends when she was a girl in Indo-China, and her feelings when Noah – the play was called Noah – said to God: 'Oh God, I wish I could speak English so that my words might reach you more quickly.' Her American friend often reproached her with speaking badly and taught her a word in which she rejoiced: 'overwhelming'. When he says it she feels like dancing – though she can't dance.

She didn't know that this taste for voices would lead her to a passionate love for music and above all for those female voices that carry one off to the ends of the earth. When she had set off for Roscoff she had not been able to bear listening to music. When she returns to the rue Poissonnière, she will listen to it and think of him. They will share Elisabeth, Erna, Gundula and all those male voices that are half-way between angels and women.

XXXV

When the young woman arrives, the old gentleman is already at the landing stage. His back makes her heart beat. His back is no longer for Madame Olive, his back is for their journey to Batz Island.

She has always liked backs. Even when she was - or thought she was - unhappy, even when they realized that things were no longer possible (physically) betwen them. She loved to snuggle up to him. Backs constitute a refusal that is not total. Backs are havens before despair. She hasn't kissed a back for months, perhaps years. She will kiss Clemenceau's back.

The old gentleman turns round. He hands her a ticket. He has a cap on.

- We've missed the half past one. We'll get the next.

She clenches the ticket in her hand. This ticket is her talisman. The pleasure boat is called *The Shooting Star*.

The young woman is going on her honeymoon to Batz Island. She is no longer on her Egyptian boat. He is no longer on the *San Diego*. He is not meeting Babaoudia at Djibouti. She is not on the *Oonas* with him.

They have barely landed on the island when a child tries

104

to sell them a lettuce. She buys it gladly. It is her wedding
bouquet. The child has fine red cheeks. She would like to kiss
it.

– What are you going to do with a lettuce at the Hotel des
Arcades?

– I'll come and eat it with you this evening.

– I don't eat much in the evenings.

– Salad is light. But we don't have to eat.

She takes his arm.

He says:

– I won't tolerate that.

The young woman removes her arm. He is difficult. She is
used to that. She has always loved difficult men. She doesn't
know what to do with her arm now.

He says:

– If you like, we can go to Madame Louise's for a
wholemeal pancake and a pitcher of cider.

She answers:

– Oh yes!

She drinks the cider in little sips. It's the first time she has
drunk cider on an island with a man. She likes this taste of
apple in her mouth. She likes Brittany, its apples and its
artichokes. If she had been the first woman, she too would
have bitten into the apple.

She remembers the time when they were still afraid of each
other and how they had come close together by means of
shots of Calvados in a café in the rue de Lappe. She
remembers their hangover the following morning: a lead
weight on their heads. He had said: 'I shall never touch

105

another drop of Calvados in my life.' She thinks he has kept his word. She sometimes drinks Calvados with the woman friend she loves, and who gets it from Normandy. She also drinks it at that other friend's, whom she also loves but who doesn't drink at all. The young woman moistens her lips in a Calvados that is now more than ten years old. But she never orders Calvados in a restaurant. Yet she has ordered just about every liqueur possible (damson, plum, raspberry) during her past life, in order to make her actions more supple, to be free from the profound timidity which is physical as well as psychological with her. She even remembers having drunk Cognac – which she can't stand – with her husband in the south of Spain – Fundador if they had it, or Carlos III, she can't remember exactly. It was during his first journey with her, to Almeria, that he got the psychological shock – not yet sexual – from that which he would be searching for in Africa.

Spanish poverty at that time, in the south, was like colonial wretchedness. The flies of Carthagena were African flies. The flies of misfortune on the eyes of children with trachoma.

The nights at Carthagena were of a frenzied gaiety. And when day broke and they saw from the window of the Hotel Alfonso XIII where they had been given a huge room with four beds – and she remembers that they had made love on each one of these beds – the waste ground, the hovels, the dust, the rags out to dry, her heart was pained, confronted with what was only a portent of the unbearable poverty they were to see a few years later from the top of the Ibn-el-Touloun mosque and she wondered where their night-time companions got the strength to laugh.

106

She says:

   – I like the taste of apples with you.

He answers:

   – I think it's time to go back.

She says:

   – I like being with you.

He answers:

   – You're not hard to please.

   She would like to say: 'I love you', but she knows that the time is not right.

XXXVI

She got him drunk on Muscadet. She drank too. Not for confrontation, but to become oblivious of herself. Alcohol makes actions more supple. It liberates bodies. It also breaks down all the barriers that people erect during the course of their lives. She is getting her way. She gets into bed fully dressed, presses against him under the sheets. He is wearing only an undershirt. A sign of youthfulness. She starts to caress him. He murmurs:

– I'm already over the hill.

She has been over the hill for a long time. She's on the other side. The other side is finding out that someone who can no longer desire you remains ineffable. She has time to tell herself (over the Muscadet) that it is better to think that he can no longer desire you physiologically. Rather than in the head and the body. Earlier he had said to her in the kitchen:

– I've been making love for sixty years, I started at the age of twelve. So you see it doesn't bother me that much these days.

– Your skin is so soft there.

How is it that that skin remains soft until the end of time?

She is on a real boat. She is sailing. She is making headway.

– You won't get your way.

She mustn't tell him that she's got it already. For her the aim was to be lying next to someone, the aim was to be lying next to him.

All the same she says:

– I know I'm not your sort. Agatha was blonde and hid behind a sunshade and Babaoudia was black.

He smiles.

– Babaoudia, who told you about Babaoudia?

– You did.

XXXVII

When the young woman goes into the beach hut that morning, she is happy. She goes in as if it were her house. She looks more closely at Agatha behind her sunshade. In Agatha's eyes she sees all that she refused him at first: tenderness, anguish. She also sees the boredom in Agatha's eyes as she helped little Marie with her homework. She sees her suffering when Armand no longer loved her – when she no longer loved him – and she sees how impossible it was for her to tell the old gentleman – who was still young – that it was him she loved. She sees her wasting away in Roscoff, waiting for her sailor husband perched in her dreams on the *San Diego*. That sailor husband who collected butterflies as blue as his eyes. He made pictures with them, amazing pictures. The sea, the look in people's eyes, mother of pearl. He hasn't talked to her about them.

In the Roscoff museum is Jean Ferry's Blue Butterfly Collection. Jean's blue is a bit like Van Gogh's yellow. He won't tell her about it but in order to achieve such colours, one must extrude one's own suffering. She would like to tell Agatha that in a modest way she replaced her last night, that she occupied the place – still warm – in the love that he bore her, in his guilt at having been unfaithful to her with Babaoudia, that she sailed a great distance in their great wooden bed, that enormous bed that is unbearable when one is on one's own. She would like to thank Agatha for not being there. Then she looks at Babaoudia who became a prostitute at the age of sixteen in order to bring up her sons. One of them is a primary school teacher in Antony, the second is a nurse at the Salpêtrière hospital, the third is a street sweeper. They left Africa that could no longer feed them thanks to Babaoudia who paid their fare.

In the bathing hut the young woman thinks of Babaoudia, then looks at the perfect face of Danielle Darrieux who has kept her eternal youth. Actors and those who died before the age of thirty possess eternal youth. The young woman kisses Agatha, Babaoudia and Danielle Darrieux. They don't turn their heads away like the old gentleman who defends his lips like a young girl. Perhaps simply because after a certain age the lips are no longer the vehicle of emotion. How can one know? How can one learn something new everyday?

Nevertheless, she has the impression that he has seen her in Roscoff two or three times. Two or three times should suffice for a life time, that should suffer for a cure. The young woman smiles: she has written 'suffer' instead of 'suffice'.

She gets undressed now. In the speckled mirror she tries to look at that body that has made love. She thinks she doesn't look bad. When it comes to it, people are nearly always more handsome naked than dressed. She runs her hands over her body. She has turned slightly golden. The Britanny sun lasts longer than elsewhere. Who is going to see that she is golden?

111

Perhaps only the mirror in her bathroom. And then? She need only smile at herself in the mirror in the rue Poissonnière where she will at last return. 'You are beautiful.' 'I like you.' The words will come back to her together with the strength to live.

The young woman comes out of the hut. He is there.

She lies down on the sand and says:

– I'm going back to Paris. Tomorrow.

He answers:

– You've got a tan.

– I think I'm going to write a book. Thanks to you.

– A book?

– A book called 'The Bathing Huts'. A book about us.

He looks at her with his great blue eyes.

– 'The Bathing Huts' is a nice title.

– I'd like to tell you something.

– Don't say it.

The young woman knows he is right. She lowers her eyes in a girlish manner. Between them they are over a hundred years old. Such sweetness.